Stin

Megan McDonald illustrated by

K
and the World's Worst Super-Stinky Sneakers

:ter H. Reynolds

CANDLEWICK PRESS

First paperback edition 2008

The Library of Congress has cataloged
the hardcover edition as follows:

McDonald, Megan.
Stink and the world's worst super-stinky sneakers /
Megan McDonald ; illustrated by Peter H. Reynolds. —1st ed.
p. cm.
Summary: A class visit to the Gross-Me-Out exhibit at the science museum inspires Stink Moody to create a variety of terrible smells to put on the sneakers he plans to enter in the World's Worst Super-Stinky Sneaker contest.
ISBN 978-0-7636-2834-5 (hardcover)
[1. Smell—Fiction. 2. Contests—Fiction. 3. Humorous stories.]
I. Reynolds, Peter, date, ill. II. Title.
PZ7.M1487Sti 2007
[Fic]—dc22 2006052585

ISBN 978-0-7636-3669-2 (paperback)

10 11 12 13 14 LBM 14 13 12 11 10 9 8

Printed in Melrose Park, IL, U.S.A.

This book was typeset in Stone Informal
with hand lettering by Peter H. Reynolds.
The illustrations were created digitally.

Candlewick Press
99 Dover Street
Somerville, Massachusetts 02144

visit us at www.candlewick.com

For Eric and Luke

M. M.

To three "big kids" who still remember what it's like to be a kid: Jess Brallier, David Samuelson, and Barry Cronin

P. H. R.

CONTENTS

GROSS
ME OUT

Gross me out!

Stink-o!

Skunksville!

Stink Moody was in love. In love with school, that is. It was the best day ever of second grade, the best day ever for Class 2D, and maybe possibly the best day ever in the whole world and his entire life so far.

Mrs. D. was taking Stink Moody and his class on a field trip. A *smell* trip. To the smelliest place on earth!

Class 2D was going on a special trip to the Gross-Me-Out exhibit at the science museum. And Stink had a fifth sense that it was going to be the smelliest field trip ever.

Stink carpooled with his two best not-smelly friends, Webster and Sophie of the Elves (a.k.a. Elizabeth, but nobody was allowed to call her that).

"Hey, guys. Did you know one human being person can smell about ten thousand smells? Also, smelling peppermint makes you smarter."

"No way, no how," said Webster.

"I love peppermint ice cream!" said

Sophie. "So I guess that makes me smart."

"How do you know so much about smelly stuff, anyway?" asked Webster.

"His name's STINK, isn't it?" said Sophie.

"No, c'mon. For real," said Webster.

"Don't forget I read the whole entire *S* encyclopedia. Books do not lie. Especially the encyclopedia."

* * *

Class 2D followed their teacher into the museum. Stink ducked as he stepped through a pair of ugly red lips and giant chomping teeth at the entrance to the wonderful world of smelly stuff.

Slimy! Oozy! Stinky! Gooey! There were beeps and toots and blinking lights in every direction. Where to start? The Vomit Machine? Musical Farts? The Burp-O-Meter?

Stink could not decide. "I think there's a giant nose here somewhere," he told his friends. "I saw the picture in the paper."

GROSS-ME-OUT
THE WONDERFUL WORLD OF
SMELLY STUFF
TICKETS
REST ROOMS
JUST SAY "AWW" OR "EWWW!"

"Count me out," said Webster. "Where there's a giant nose, there could be—"

"Giant BOOGERS!" said Sophie and Webster at the same time, shivering at the thought.

"Well, I'm *going* to check out the giant nose *first*," said Stink.

"Not me," said Webster.

"Not me," said Sophie.

"Okay, *smell* you around!" Stink said, cracking himself up.

Stink's STINKY FACTS!
RACE YA!
SNEEZES TRAVEL AS FAST AS A CAR!
40 MILES PER HOUR
THE FASTEST SNEEZE CLOCKED IN AT 100 MPH.
ACHOOOO!!
SNEEZE-BLASTER 3000
NO LIE.

More Fun than Earwax

Stink took an up-close-and-personal tour of the giant nose. He got attacked by giant nose hairs, peered down a big ugly bumpy throat, and skipped through the Hall of Mucus. He even learned how boogers are made—not pretty!

"Having fun?" Mrs. D. asked him.

"Are you kidding? This is more fun than earwax!" Stink told Mrs. D. "And educational, too," he added. Grown-ups loved the *e* word. They liked to think you were learning stuff no matter what.

Mrs. D. smiled. "Stink, you seem to be interested in the sense of smell. Maybe you'd like to try the Everybody Stinks exhibit? Nobody else seems to want to go near it."

Mrs. D. pinched her nose and shook her head.

"How smelly can it be?" Stink said bravely. Mrs. D. pointed to the far end of the exhibit. Stink strolled over and read the instructions.

"Match the body odor with the body parts they come from," Stink read aloud. Before Stink knew it, the whole class had gathered around.

Webster announced to the class, "Hey, everybody! Stink's going to smell B.O.!" Stink wasn't so sure he wanted to smell B.O. But he hated to let Webster and everybody down. So Stink mustered up all his courage, leaned over, put his nose right up to the bottle, and squeezed.

He took one sniff, then scrunched up his face, clutched his chest, and crumpled to the floor.

"Uhh!" everybody gasped, taking in what sounded like one big breath.

WHAT'S THAT SMELL?
ARMPIT
ROTTEN EGG
SKUNK
COME T
VO
FLATULENCE FESTIVAL
VAT OF SALIVA
SQUEEZE THE BOTTLE and SNIFF DEEPLY

"Ha, ha, ha! Gotcha!" Stink cried, jumping back up.

"What did it smell like?" Sophie asked.

"Feet!" said Stink. "It's not that bad. Just smells like dirty socks when your feet sweat and you take your shoes off."

"Sounds bad to me," said Webster.

Stink squeezed the next bottle. "Uck. This one smells like onion. Maybe garlic. Phew! Bad breath," Stink said, waving his hand in front of his face. "P.U. This one smells like my soccer shirt! Armpit alert!"

"It's B.O.!" somebody shouted. "He did it! He really smelled B.O.! And he didn't even faint!"

After Stink smelled all the body-part smells, he moved to the next station. Rotten eggs! Dirt! Perfume! Moth balls! Skunk! Rotten cabbage! Dog breath! Old fish! Dead broccoli?

Stink sniffed and snuffled his way through a dozen yucky, rotten smells. He made a few faces, but he guessed every single smell right.

"P.U.! How do you do that? You didn't miss one!" said Webster.

"I just follow my nose," said Stink, sticking his expert sniffer in the air.

"You always were nosy," said Sophie of the Elves, laughing.

"Some people have an excellent sense of smell," Mrs. D. explained.

"I smell something, too," said Sophie. "Hamburgers!"

"When do we eat lunch?" asked Webster. "My digestion is empty."

* * *

Class 2D sat at the picnic tables outside, munching on sandwiches. Mrs. D. passed around flyers from the museum about a stinky sneaker contest being held at the park in two weeks.

Stink read the flyer.

"Wow! Check it out! Can anybody enter?"

"Anybody with smelly sneakers," said Mrs. D., chuckling.

MUSEUM

"Stink's are the *WORST,*" said Webster, backing away from Stink.

"But my sneakers are so smelly I had to wear rain boots today," said Sophie, showing off her pink polka-dot boots. "I bet I can win."

"My sneakers will beat the pants off yours any day," Stink told Sophie.

"But you haven't even smelled mine," said Sophie.

Stink shrugged. "I'm just *saying.*" His sneakers just *had* to be the smelliest. But what if Sophie's were super-stinky bad, too? Or worse?

"Well, I'm sure my daughter will want to enter the 'Smell Monsters,'" Mrs. D. said, making air quotes with her hands. "That's what we call *her* sneakers. So, I hope to see some of you there in two weeks." Then Mrs. D. asked them all about what they learned at the Gross-Me-Out exhibit.

"I learned that even walruses have dandruff," said Eliza.

"I learned the words to the diarrhea song," said Patrick.

"Let's wait till AFTER lunch to hear that," said Mrs. D.

"I learned how to say *fart* in Spanish," said Jordan. "'*Pedo.*'"

"I learned that spit is gross," said Riley.

"I learned that there are more critters in your mouth than people in Australia," said Sophie of the Elves.

"I learned that Stink is the best smeller in the world!" said Webster.

"We should call you The Nose," said Sophie. "You know how to smell better than a dog."

“Better than an ant!” said Stink. Everybody looked at him funny. “What? An ant has five noses,” said Stink, nodding his head and tapping his honker. “No lie!”

STINK'S STINKY FACTS!

A QUARTER MILLION STINKERS!

DID YOU KNOW THAT JUST ONE FOOT CONTAINS 250,000 SWEAT GLANDS AND OOZES UP TO TWO CUPS OF SWEAT — Every day?

NO WONDER SNEAKERS ARE SO SMELLY!

Rumpel-STINK-skin

I'm home!" Stink called, bursting through the front door.

"How was your field trip?" Mom asked.

"You mean my *smell* trip!" said Stink. He reached into his backpack and handed his mom the flyer for the smelly sneaker contest.

"I think it really stinks that Stink got to go to the Stinky Museum and I didn't," said his big sister, Judy.

"It was so way fun. And gross. I learned a ton of smelly stuff."

"Like what?" Judy asked.

"Like everybody has their own smell, except if you're twins. And guess what? We can smell stuff even when we're sleeping, and, oh yeah, a boy moth can smell a girl moth a block away."

"Mr. Nose-It-All," said Judy.

Stink stuck his expert sniffer in the air. "Is something burning?"

"Ack!" said Mom, rushing to the kitchen and whisking the skillet off the stove top. She waved her hand through the smoke. "I was making toasted cheese sandwiches for you kids."

"And now your cheese sandwiches are toast," said Judy, cracking herself up.

"Good thing you smelled something, Stink," said Mom.

"Human Smoke Alarm!" said Judy.

"At the museum, kids were calling me The Nose," said Stink, tapping his right nostril. "I found out today that I can smell stuff really, really great, better than anybody in my whole class. Sophie says I smell better than a dog."

"I should hope so!" said Mom. Mom and Judy cracked up.

"Woof!" said Stink.

"And here I thought you just had a nose for *trouble,"* said Mom.

"Laugh all you want," said Stink. "But this nose could make me famous."

"My elbow's famous," said Judy, holding up the elbow that once starred in a picture in the newspaper.

"No, I mean it. When I grow up, I'm going to do something great with this nose." said Stink. "You can't waste a nose like this." He admired himself in the mirror, turning his head from left to right and studying The Nose, his best feature.

"You could be a circus freak!" said

Judy. "Like that guy with the seven-and-a-half-inch-long nose!"

"No, I mean like a professional smeller."

"I thought you wanted to be president of your own candy store."

"That was before *The Nose,*" said Stink.

"What happened to being an inventor?" asked Mom.

"I can still invent stuff. Like an alarm clock that wakes you up *with a smell.*"

"There's no such job as a Smeller, is there, Mom?" Judy asked.

"I don't really know," said Mom. "Maybe you could work for a perfume company. Or you could test smells for new products."

"I have a smell test," said Judy. "Cover your eyes with a blindfold, and I'll find smelly stuff and see if you can guess what it is. It's called . . . the Way-Official Moody Stink-a-Thon."

"Easy!" said Stink. The two kids ran upstairs. Judy got a bandanna and tied it nice and snug over Stink's eyes. She held the end of a pencil under his nose.

"Rubbery. Smells like a pencil. . . . Eraser!" said Stink.

"Aw!" Judy picked up a marker from Stink's desk.

Sniff, sniff. "Smelly marker. Red."

"You peeked!" said Judy.

"Did not!"

"Did too! Nobody can smell colors. Not even Mr. Nose-It-All."

"Yah-huh. It's watermelon flavored."

Judy held up a bubble gum comic. Stink sniffed several times. He thought. He sniffed again. "Bubble gum."

"WRONG!" said Judy. "Bubble gum *comic.*"

"No fair!" said Stink.

Judy went and got her Venus flytrap. Stink sniffed the air once. Twice. "Jaws!" he said, grinning.

"How did you know?" asked Judy. "Venus flytraps don't smell."

"They do if they've been eating raw hamburger. And dead flies."

"Hold on. Wait right there." Judy ran downstairs and came back with more stuff to smell. One by one she held them up to Stink's nose.

"Pepper!" said Stink. "Ah-choo!" he

FOOT BALL FEST
SPACE PILOT
DARE
STOTT'S Coffee
CAPTAIN COSMIC SLACKS

sneezed. "Dad's coffee. *Bluck!* Lemon. Stinky cheese. Week-old pizza."

"WOW!" said Judy. "You even got the week-old pizza. I know you're peeking."

"No way! I swear on Toady," said Stink.

"This time I'm REALLY going to stump you. Ready?"

"Ready," said Stink, sticking his nose up in the air. Judy held out the secret, smelly, Stink-stumping odorific object.

"P.U.!" said Stink. "It's worse than smelly sneakers. Worse than dirty socks.

Worse than a skunk. It smells like one-hundred-year-old barf."

"Wrong!" said Judy.

"Is it two-hundred-year-old buffalo dung?"

"Nope."

"Is it a stinky baby diaper?"

"N-O!"

"Is it—*sniff, sniff, sniff*—eggs? One-thousand-year-old rotten eggs?"

"Rumpelstiltskin!" said Judy. "How'd you guess it was stinky old eggs?"

"You mean I guessed it? For real?" Stink yanked off his blindfold. Lumpy clumps of something disgusting were in Mouse's cat food dish.

"It *is* rotten eggs," said Judy. "Beef-and-scrambled-eggs cat food. Mouse won't eat the egg part."

"Just call me Rumpel-STINK-skin," said Stink, cracking himself up. Judy cracked up, too.

“So, did I pass the smell test?”

“With flying colors!” said Judy. “You truly live up to the name *Stink.* From this day forward, you will be known as Rumpel-Stink-Skin, Grand Prize Winner of the Way-Official Moody Stink-a-Thon.”

“What’s my prize?” asked Stink.

“No prize,” said Judy. “Just the satisfaction of knowing how smelly you are.”

“That really stinks,” said Stink.

Stink's STINKY FACTS!
Who NEEDS A NOSE?
SMELLS YUMMY!
A SNAKE HAS A SMELLY TONGUE (A TONGUE TO SMELL WITH, THAT IS).
FLIES SMELL WITH THEIR FEET!
GROSS!
SNIFF! SLURP!
Believe it or Not, an Octopus smells with its eyes! It has smell receptors located right behind those Bulgy peepers!

TOILET WATER

Stink printed a page from his favorite website called "The Science of Stink" and ran to show his family.

"Hey, guys!" said Stink. "What's taller than a man, smells worse than roadkill, and looks like the color of blood?"

"An elephant painting a picture?" asked Judy.

"No way," said Stink.

"Is it the Abominable Smell Man?" asked Judy. "Frankenstein Valentine?"

"Can somebody else guess, please?" asked Stink.

"I'm still thinking," said Mom.

"Let's see," said Dad. "How about . . . Santa Claus driving a garbage truck?"

"No," said Stink. "I'll give you a hint. It's something Mom likes a real lot."

"Are you sure?" Mom asked. "I can't imagine liking anything that smells like roadkill."

"Give up? It's a corpse flower!" cried Stink. "World's smelliest flower. It says so right here." Stink showed his family the full-color photo of Trudy the Titan.

"Rare!" said Judy. "It says it only blooms a few times in its life, and it stinks worse than rotten eggs for about three days."

"Worse than rotten fish and rotting pumpkins, too," said Mom. "Phew!"

"Insects like it, though," said Dad, reading over Stink's shoulder.

"They can have it," said Mom.

"And look here," Stink said, pointing to the bottom of the page. "It says scientists come from all over the country to take samples of Trudy's perfume and bottle some up. Mom, you were right. That's something I could do with my nose."

"Make stinky perfume?" asked Judy.

"I meant be a scientist," said Stink. "You know, I'd get to sniff out rare smelly flowers and study them and stuff."

"Bluck," said Judy. "It says here, in

the first ten hours, the corpse flower smells as bad as an outhouse. Or dead elephants. Do you really want to smell dead elephants for a living, Stink?"

"Well, stinky perfume's a good idea, too," said Stink.

"In my day we called it toilet water," said Mom.

"I'm serious, Mom," said Stink.

"I'm not kidding!" said Mom. "You can buy it at the store. It's just like perfume, only watered down a bit. And they call it *Eau de Toilette.*"

"Is that French for Odor of Toilet?" asked Stink, cracking up.

"Something like that," Mom said.

"But who'd wear stinky perfume on purpose?" asked Judy.

"Same people who pay a lot of money for toilet water," said Stink. Dad couldn't help snickering at that one.

"A person could wear stinky perfume

to scare off vampires," said Stink. "Or better yet, big sisters. Judy cooties!"

"Hardee-har-har," said Judy.

"All I need now are a few dead elephants," said Stink.

STINK'S STINKY FACTS!
WHAT'S THE BIG STINK?
IT SMELLS LIKE ROADKILL AND LOOKS LIKE ROTTING MEAT. IT HAS SOME OF THE SAME CHEMICALS AS A DEAD BODY. IT ONLY BLOOMS FOR ABOUT THREE DAYS. . . .
IT'S THE WORLD'S LARGEST, STINKIEST FLOWER—
THE CORPSE FLOWER!!
UGH!

Eau de CORPSE FLOWER

On Saturday morning, Stink could not wait to start his new career. He set up his lab in the kitchen sink. He laid out tweezers and eyedroppers on a towel. He lined up ten empty little spice jars on the counter. He collected a whole jar of real toilet water—*from the toilet!*

Perfect!

The doorbell rang. "Hi, Eliz—I mean, Sophie of the Elves," Judy said. "C'mon in. Dr. Franken-stink is in his lab. Stink! Your friend with the funny name is here!"

Stink came out of the kitchen wearing Mom's apron and green rubber scrub gloves. "Hi, Sophie," said Stink.

"Stink's making stinky perfume," Judy explained, drawing circles in the air for the cuckoo sign.

"Want to help?" Stink asked.

"Sure," said Sophie. "I like making magic potions and stuff."

"Magic potions!" said Judy. "You mean *love* potions?"

"Let's go," said Stink. "Maybe we can make some potions that turn big sisters into warthogs."

✶ ✶ ✶

Back in the Franken-stink lab, Stink got out Mom's measuring cups and spoons. Sophie stirred together spices and food coloring. "Are you entering the smelly sneaker contest next Saturday?" she asked Stink.

"Definitely," said Stink.

"Me too," Sophie said.

Stink looked down at Sophie's sneakers. They were bad, all right. Her toe poked out of one, the laces were almost black, and the tongues hung sideways, worse than a slobbery dog.

"They smell like a swamp!" said Stink, even though he knew his stinkers could beat hers any day.

"And these aren't even my worst pair!" Sophie grinned.

Uh-oh, thought Stink.

"Well, I sure hope one of us wins," Sophie said.

"Yeah, and I hope the one of us is me!" Stink joked.

"Here, add some toilet water," Stink said, pouring the water from the toilet into the blender. They added green pickle juice. They added P.U. garlic. They added slimy dead-flower water.

"Disgusting," said Sophie, staring at the oogey green murk in the blender.

"What else stinks around here?" asked Stink.

"Besides you?" said Judy, walking past the kitchen.

"Hardee-har-har," said Stink.

"This potion smells bad, but it's not even close to corpse flower," said Stink.

He ran upstairs and came back in a flash, holding up a small, amber glass vial. "Toad food!"

"Tofu?" asked Sophie. "Tofu doesn't smell."

"No, *toad* food. Actually, it's dead shrimp eggs from my science kit. Even Toady won't eat it."

Stink shook the bottle till it was

empty, then pushed the buttons on the blender. *Mix. Whip. Puree. LIQUEFY!* Stink and Sophie watched the twisting tornado of green gunk whip itself into a frothy frenzy.

OFF! "Perfect!" said Stink, peering into the foaming blender.

In no time, they had ten whole

bottles of putrid perfumes lined up and down the counter.

"Let's label them and give them names," said Stink. "How about *Eau de Corpse Flower*? It's French."

"Essence of Toad," said Sophie.

"Venus de Stinko," said Stink.

Just then, Mouse crept into the

kitchen. She took one whiff, let out a yowl, and bolted outside through the cat door.

Stink handed Sophie an eyedropper. "Help me fill this little vial," said Stink. Sophie squeezed the last drops from the blender into the teeny tiny bottle, then screwed the cap back on. She helped Stink tie a piece of string around it, looping it over his neck.

"What are you going to do with this stinky perfume?" asked Sophie of the Elves. "Keep away vampires?"

"Keep away sisters!" said Stink.

Stink's STINKY FACTS!
WANT TO SMELL LIKE THE CIRCUS?
TRY A PERFUME CALLED ZZING. SOON YOU'LL BE WEARING THE ZING OF PEANUTS, SAWDUST, AND... ELEPHANTS!
Zzing
IF YOU WANT TO SMELL LIKE A TREE, THERE'S A PERFUME FOR THAT TOO. OR CANDY. OR... BELIEVE IT OR NOT... DIRT! EEWWW!!
TREE
Candy
DIRT

Unidentified Flying Odor

P.U.!" said Judy, coming into Stink's room. "Did you take a bath in that stinky perfume or something?"

"Or something," said Stink.

"Then I hate to tell you, but you have a UFO in your room."

"Do not," said Stink.

"Not the alien kind of UFO," said Judy. "An Unidentified Flying Odor. I can smell it from my room."

Stink kicked his sneakers under the bed.

"Stink, it's those sneakers. You're stinking up the whole house with those yucks. You have to get them out of here."

Stink tossed his sneakers into the hallway.

"That's even closer," said Judy. "I can already smell them up on my top bunk! Even Mouse is about to pass out from the fumes."

Stink went back to his desk and scribbled on a piece of paper. He came out into the hallway and tacked up a sign over his sneakers:

"Ha, ha, very funny. Like that really helped," said Judy, pinching her nose closed and talking in a funny voice.

"Then just shut your door," said Stink. "Like this!" He slammed the door on purpose.

Stink heard Judy stomp into the bathroom. Stink heard Judy slam the medicine cabinet door. Stink heard Judy rattle around in the hall.

Stink could not concentrate on drawing comics. He could not read the *T-for-Toads* encyclopedia. He could not hear himself think with all that stomping and slamming and rattling.

Stink opened his door.

A cloud of white dust attacked him. He coughed and waved his hand in front of his face. Stink could hardly see his sister. Judy had powder in her hair and on her face and all the way down to her shoes. She looked like a human marshmallow. She looked like the Abominable Snow Girl. She looked like a cumulonimbus cloud.

"What's with all the powder?" Stink asked, still coughing. Then the cloud cleared. The dust settled. And Stink saw it.

"OH, NO!" screamed Stink. "My sneakers! My beautiful super-smelly sneakers!"

"It's okay," said Judy. "The powder will help. It'll soak up the smell and they won't stink so bad."

"NO! You don't get it!" said Stink.

Beware!
Hall of FUMES

"I was stinking them up on purpose, so I could enter them in the All-Time, World's Worst, Super-Stinky Sneaker Contest. How could you not know that? How could you forget?"

"Oops!" said Judy.

Stink did not know what to do. Now his perfectly smelly sneakers were not perfect at all. They were perfect for winning an air-freshener contest. They were perfect for winning a not-stinky perfume contest. No way were they going to beat Sophie *now.*

"Go get Mom," said Stink. "It's an

emergency. A super-stinky sneaker emergency."

"Trust me, Stink. All the powder in the world could not make those puppies smell good again. They smell even worse now, if you ask me. Kind of sweet, but kind of sour. Sweet and Sour Sneakers! I mean, they still make me gag and almost want to barf."

"*Almost* is not good enough to win," said Stink. "They have to have at least a double-gag factor. A triple-quadruple barf factor."

"Why don't we just smell them up more?" asked Judy. "Operation Smelly

Sneakers. We could pour vinegar on them. Or pickle juice! We could throw them in the garbage for a while. Wait. I know. I got it!" Judy snapped her fingers. "We could use a bottle of your stinky perfume!"

"That would be cheating," said Stink. "The rules say you have to stink them up by wearing them. Pickle juice is illegal. Garbage doesn't count. And stinky perfume is definitely against the rules."

"Do the rules say what to do if your big sister goofs up?"

"The rules say you better run!" said

Stink. He chased his sister down the hall and into the bathroom and out of the bathroom and down the stairs and into the kitchen and around the table, holding out his vial of anti-sister stinky perfume all the while.

WALKING SPAGHETTI?

POWDER MAY HELP STINKY SNEAKERS, BUT IF YOU GET SPRAYED BY A SKUNK, MOST PEOPLE WILL TELL YOU TO TAKE A BATH IN TOMATO JUICE!

DOES IT WORK? NOT REALLY — BUT YOUR NOSE **WILL** GET TIRED OF SMELLING SKUNK AND START SMELLING TOMATO, SO AT LEAST YOU'LL **THINK** IT WORKS!

TOMATO

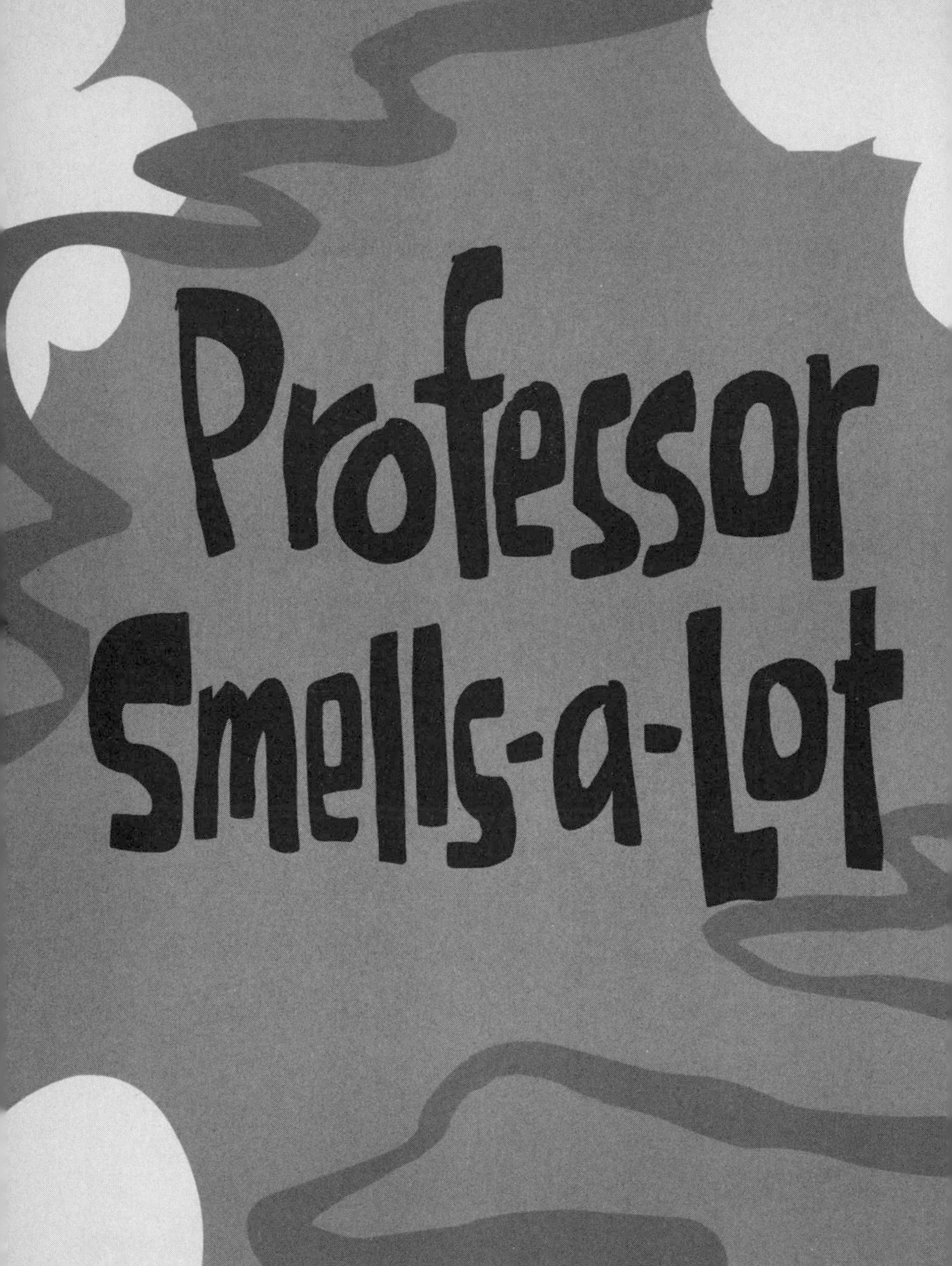
Professor
Smells-a-Lot

Next Saturday morning, Stink woke up to the most wonderful smell. Not pancakes cooking. Not bacon frying. The yucky, blucky putrid stench of smelly sneakers. Sweet! His sneakers were wonderfully smelly again. Back to where they were before his sister-the-human-marshmallow went powder crazy and made them smell sweet as roses.

Stink was going to win the All-Time, World's Worst, Super-Stinky Sneaker

Contest for sure. And today was the big day. His moment to shine. His moment to *stink*!

"What's that smell?" Dad asked at breakfast. "Don't tell me Mouse dragged another dead critter in here."

"It's him," said Judy, pointing to her brother. "Stink, you reek."

"YOU-reek-a!" said Stink. "Get it? Eureka!"

"I get it that you smell," said Judy.

"Stink's entering a rotten sneaker contest today," Mom explained to Dad.

"Interesting," said Dad.

"My teacher's going to be there,"

Stink told them. "She said if I come early, I'll be able to meet somebody interesting."

"It's probably just a guy dressed up like a giant sneaker or something," said Judy.

"Or something," said Stink.

"Mom, Dad? Can I go, too?" Judy asked. "Just to watch, I mean."

"Let's all go," said Dad.

"But only if we put the smelly sneakers in the trunk, right, Dad?" said Judy.

* * *

When Stink got to the contest, Webster and Sophie of the Elves came running up to him. "There's no contest!" said Webster.

"What?" asked Stink. "What do you mean? I know it's today."

"One of the judges caught a cold and he can't smell right," said Sophie. "So they had to cancel the contest."

"No way."

"Yah-huh. Mrs. D. said! I'm not even in the contest, but I feel bad for you and Sophie," Webster told his friend.

Stink could not believe his stinky,

awful, no-good, very bad luck. "You mean I wore the same socks for six days and slept in my sneakers and tromped through mud puddles and swamp water for nothing?"

Just then, Stink saw his teacher. "Mrs. D.!" called Stink. "Is it true? There's really not going to be a stinky sneaker contest?"

"Well," said Mrs. D., "we might have a way to save the day."

"Really?" everybody asked.

"Stink, when we heard one of the judges was sick, I thought, who else do we know who just might have an

TICKETS

amazing, incredible sense of smell? And right away I thought of you, Stink Moody, The Nose."

"Stink could be a judge!" said Webster.

"What do you say, Stink?" asked Mrs. D.

"Me? A judge? For real? You mean I, Stink Moody, get to be a real-and-true professional smeller?"

"Just call him Professor Smells-a-Lot," said Judy.

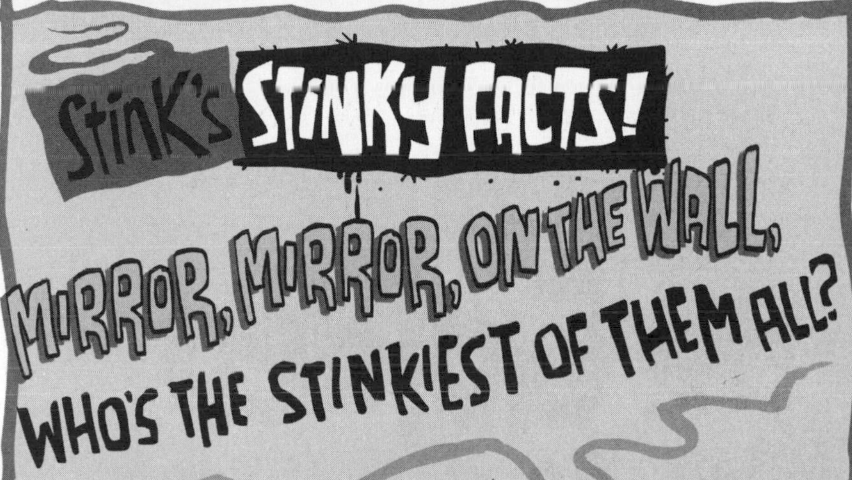

SKUNK SPRAY CONTAINS THE SAME CHEMICAL AS ROTTEN EGGS, GARLIC, AND COFFEE!

STINKBUGS ARE THE SMELLIEST BUGS AROUND. ONE KIND OF STINKBUG CAN "SPIT" ITS SMELLY STUFF UP TO 12 INCHES. NOT BAD FOR SUCH A LITTLE GUY!

The Golden Clothespin Award

In the middle of the park stood a big red-and-white-striped circus tent with a banner that said:

"Dad and I will wander around and meet you kids back here later," said Mom.

Stink opened the flaps and stepped through the tent door. *Phew!* A great wall of smell almost knocked him over. It was like standing smack-dab in the middle of a cloud—a giant, invisible, cumulonimbus stink cloud. Worse than thirty dead elephants. Worse than sixty corpse flowers. Worse than ninety-nine bottles of toilet water.

Lined up on tables all around the tent were dozens of putrid sneakers. Each pair had a number, so nobody

SMELL
91
92
93
94
95
96
97
98
99
100

would know who owned which sneakers. Stink took his smelly shoes out of the bag and set them on the table.

"You'll be number twenty-seven," said a lady behind the table.

"Stink!" said Judy. "You can't enter your own shoes in the contest."

"Why not?" Stink asked.

"Don't you get it? You're a judge now. Judges can't win the contest. That's like voting for yourself for president."

"So?"

"Stink, would you think it was fair if

I were a judge, and I picked my own sneakers to win?"

"Not really," said Stink.

"See? Picking your own sneakers makes you a cheater head."

"A cheese head?" asked Stink.

"No, a big fat *Cheater* Head," Judy said.

Just then, Mrs. D. motioned for Stink to come over to the important table up front, where the judges sat. Red and blue ribbons were set out on a fancy tablecloth, alongside the shiny Golden Clothespin trophy.

"What's with the fancy clothespin?" whispered Judy.

"That's the award," said Stink, pinching his nose shut, like with a clothespin, and making a P.U. face.

"Here's your new judge," Mrs. D. told the other two judges. "Meet James Moody. Believe it or not, he goes by the name Stink."

The other two judges laughed. "Well, your name alone qualifies you to be a judge," said the woman from Odor-

Munchers. "Thanks, Stink. You really saved the day."

"Glad to meet you. I'm Mr. Moore. Call me Steve," said the other judge.

"You sure are tall," said Stink, shaking his hand.

"Stink," said Mrs. D., "this is the man I wanted you to meet. Mr. Moore—I mean, Steve—is a professional smeller."

"That's me," said Steve.

"You mean that's your job—you smell stuff?" asked Stink.

"That's my job. I work for NASA, and they call me the Master Sniffer."

"They call me The Nose!" said Stink excitedly. "I want to be a professional smeller when I grow up. But my sister said—"

"What kind of stuff do you smell?" Judy asked Steve.

"Anything that goes up into space, I'm your man. If it's too smelly, we can't have it aboard the space shuttle. Up there, you can't just open a window. You'd be surprised at the number of things that don't pass the smell test."

"Really? Like what?" asked Stink.

"Like film for a camera, felt-tip markers, a stuffed teddy bear . . ."

"Bad news, Stink!" said Judy. "You can't go up into space now. They won't let you take your teddy bear."

"Hardee-har-har," said Stink. Steve the Smeller laughed a deep laugh.

"What do you have to do to be a professional smeller?" Stink asked. "Do you have to be tall? Because I'm short."

"No, but you can't have allergies," said Steve. "You have to be good at detecting odors, like, say, new-car smell. And you have to be willing to sniff bad smells—even a dirty diaper."

Stink nodded like a bobble-head doll

on a dashboard. "I sniffed a whole stinky museum," Stink told him.

"And of course you have to pass a test. Every few months, I have to take the ten-bottle test."

"I made ten bottles of my own stinky toilet water!" said Stink. "Just ask my sister."

"I sniff scents in a bottle and I have to guess if it's popcorn or wet-paint smell," said Steve. "Then I rate it on a Sniff Scale from zero to four. Anything over a 2.4 on the Sniff Scale fails the test. Kind of like what we're going to do today."

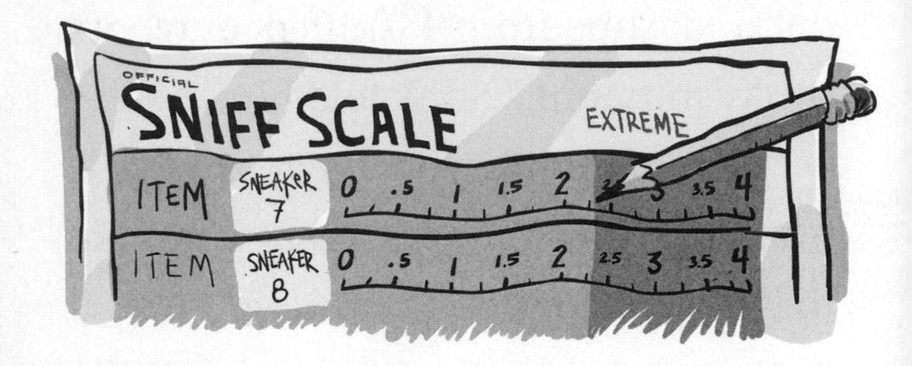

"And I passed my sister's Way-Official Moody Stink-a-Thon," Stink told him.

"Good for you," said Steve. "Sounds like you're already on your way to becoming a Master Sniffer."

"Someday I really want to smell a corpse flower."

"Oh, those corpse flowers sure are humdingers," said Steve. "I flew all the way to England once, just to smell one at the Royal Botanic Gardens."

"Whoa. No way!" Stink wanted to hear more, but it was time for the contest to begin.

Stink rushed over to smelly sneakers Number Twenty-seven. He hated to admit that Judy was right. But entering his own sneakers *was* no fair. He, Stink Moody, did not want to be the UN-proud winner of the All-Time, World's Worst, Super-Stinky *Cheater* Contest.

Stink gave the number back to the lady. “I’m not in the contest anymore,” he told her. “I’m a judge now!”

No way did Stink want to cheat. He was an official Junior Sniffer now. A Junior Sniffer could not be a big fat cheesy, cheese-head, cheater head.

CAPTAIN DIAPERS!

BELIEVE IT OR NOT, ASTRONAUTS WEAR DIAPERS ON SPACE WALKS! REAL-LIFE MASTER SNIFFERS HAVE TO SNIFF (CLEAN!) DIAPERS BEFORE THEY GO UP INTO SPACE!

WEIRD STUFF THEY'VE SNIFFED: PAINT, SHAVING CREAM, UN-YUCKY SNEAKERS, A GUITAR, BARNEY (THE STUFFED DINO), SALLY RIDE'S MAKEUP (IT DID NOT PASS THE TEST!)

World's Worst Super-Stinky CHEATER Contest

Let the sniffing begin!" said the head judge lady. She handed Stink a clipboard. He took his sniffing very seriously. He walked up and down the rows and rows of torn sneakers, worn sneakers, yucky blucky sneakers. He walked in front of the sneakers and behind the sneakers. Here a sniff, there a sniff, everywhere a sniff, sniff.

Stink rated each pair on a smelly scale of zero to four. He wrote down notes like "smells like a swamp" and "worse than a dead skunk" and "triple P.U." All the while, he couldn't help wondering which pair was Sophie's.

"Hey, I'll give you a tip." Steve the Smeller handed Stink a tissue. "Take a whiff of a pair of sneakers, then hold the tissue up to your nose in between sniffs. That way, your sense of smell won't get so tired."

"Thanks!" said Stink. Wow-ee! A professional tip from Professor Smells-a-Lot himself. Stink puffed up with pride. He sniffed the next pair.

"What do you smell?" Steve asked.

JUDGING AREA
SPACE
64

"Feet," said Stink. He did the tissue trick, then smelled the sneakers again.

"What else?" asked Steve.

"Dirt. Old carpet smell. Maybe even moldy cheese."

"Good for you," said Steve. "Moldy cheese. That's exactly what I thought."

Stink sniffed some more sneakers. He couldn't help thinking that his were still the smelliest. He couldn't help thinking that he could have won the Golden Clothespin Award. Until he came to Smelly Sneaker Pair Number Thirteen, that is.

Stink leaned over and took another

whiff. Phew! His eyes crossed; his nose wrinkled; his tongue curled.

Number Thirteen smelled worse than a barn full of bats. Worse than a basement full of rats. Number Thirteen smelled stinkier than the litter boxes of ten hundred cats!

He sniffed Number Thirteen. He sniffed the clean tissue from Steve the Smeller. Then he sniffed pair Number Thirteen again. All the toilet water in the world could not have made his shoes as smelly as these sneakers.

Stink E. Moody, Judge and Junior Sniffer, had found a real winner. A way-official, want-to-barf, gag-me-with-a-spoon winner.

"Geez, Louise," said the lady judge when she came to Number Thirteen. "Jump back, Jack. I think I'm going to pass out."

"This one's a Humpty of a Dumpty," Professor Smeller agreed.

"Rotten eggs," said the lady judge.

"Burnt hair," said Steve.

"Cat pee," said Stink. "And dead worms."

"He's got the nose, all right," said the professor. "Not many noses would pick up on that dead worm smell."

"Worse than rancid roadkill," said the lady.

"Worse than C_4H_9SeH!" said Steve.

"What's that?" asked Stink.

"Skunk spray," Steve told him. Stink cracked up.

Stink knew for sure now. These sneakers would be outlawed in outer space. These skunks were a number ten on a scale of zero to four. All the king's horses and all the bad smells could not outsmell the Numero Uno, All-Time World's Stinkiest Sneakers, Putrid Pair Number Thirteen.

* * *

Stink wrote down his final score. He turned in his clipboard. All the votes were counted.

At last it was time. Time to announce the Grand Prize Winner of the All-Time, World's Worst, Super-Stinky Sneaker Contest.

Professor Steve stepped up to the microphone. "Attention! May I have your attention, please?"

Everybody gathered around. All ears were listening. Not even a dog barked.

"We are pleased to announce the winners of the Tenth Annual All-Time, World's Worst, Super-Stinky Sneaker

SPACE
PROGRAM
WINNER

Contest. It was a close call. All sneakers in the contest were truly worthy. Truly smelly. We have two runners-up. Number Six and Number Thirty-seven, please step up to the podium."

"Number Six," he said, holding out a red ribbon. "These puppies smell worse than dog breath. Congratulations. Now get them outta here."

"Number Thirty-seven," said Steve, handing over another red ribbon, "your stinkers make a pile of garbage smell sweet. Congratulations."

Everybody clapped and cheered.

Stink could hardly wait to hear whose sneakers would take the grand prize—the Golden Clothespin.

"Now, the moment we've been waiting for. There's one pair of sneakers that all three judges gave a top score of 4+++. The Grand Prize Winner of the Golden Clothespin Award is . . . da-da-da-DA! Number Thirteen. Who has number thirteen? Please come up front to the judges' podium and claim your prizes."

"Thirteen? Did he just say thirteen? That's me!" yelled Sophie of the Elves.

She rushed up to the podium. "I can't believe it! I really won?" she asked. "Stink, how'd you know it was me?"

"I didn't!" said Stink. "Honest! I never smelled those sneakers before in my life!"

"They won fair and square," said Steve. "We smelled everything from dead worms to skunk spray on those sneakers."

"Way to go, Sophie," said Webster.

"Step right up here, young lady," said Professor Smeller. "For having the world's all-time smelliest sneakers, I award you this trophy of the Golden

Clothespin, one gift certificate for a new pair of sweet-smelling sneakers, and last but not least, one FREE trip for two to the Odor-Munchers Air Freshener factory."

"Thank you!" said Sophie, holding up her trophy. Tons of people were clapping and yelling "Woo-hoo!" A guy from the newspaper was even snapping pictures.

"Tell us," said Steve the Smeller, "what's your secret, Sophie? What makes your sneakers so smelly?"

"Simple," said Sophie. "No socks.

And when my parents make me take a bath, I hang my feet over the edge of the tub and don't wash them. Ever."

"P.U.," said Professor Smeller. "Congratulations, young lady! Your shoes will be entered into the Hall of Fumes at the community center, where hopefully they can be seen but not smelled by all."

"Can I have your autograph?" Sophie asked.

"Sure," said Steve.

"Me, too!" said Stink. "Can you sign my shoe?"

SPACE

P.U!

Professor Steve Smells-a-Lot signed Stink's smelly sneaker. *From one Master Sniffer to another,* Steve wrote.

"I'll never *ever* wash these shoes now!" said Stink.

ONE YEAR, THE WINNER HAD A SNEAKER THAT CAUSED ONE JUDGE TO GAG, ONE TO BACK AWAY, AND ONE TO NEARLY PASS OUT! GOOD THING THE PRIZE INCLUDED A NEW PAIR OF SNEAKERS!

Mr. Stinky

After the contest, Sophie of the Elves and Webster came back to Stink's house for pizza. Sophie passed the shiny Golden Clothespin trophy around for everybody to see.

"Are you sure you're not mad about the contest?" Sophie asked Stink. "I know how much you wanted to win and get the Golden Clothespin trophy and everything."

"That was before," said Stink. "Before I knew my friend was going to take me

to the air freshener factory. Hint, hint."
Sophie giggled.

"And before I got to meet Professor Smeller in person and be a Junior Sniffer for a day. He told me I have The Nose. What could be better than that? And I got something even smellier than a Golden Clothespin trophy."

"What?" asked Sophie.

"Spill it," said Webster.

"I can't spill it," said Stink. "Never, ever, ever!" He held out the vial around his neck. "In this vial is something even more vile than stinky perfume. Stinkier than C_4H_9SeH, skunk spray. Smelliest of all smells." Stink waved the open vial in front of their nostrils.

"P.U.!" Webster ran for the window. Sophie's eyes watered.

"Behold! Genuine and for-real *eau de* corpse flower. Professor Smelly went to Washington, D.C., before coming to judge the contest. And he smelled a real corpse flower named Mr. Stinky. And he got to take scientific samples. In this jar is one drop of super-stinky essence of corpse flower. No lie."

"You mean you're really going to wear that vile vial?" asked Webster.

"Always," said Stink.

Petruzziello's
PIZZA
Slice of Heaven

"Now we're going to have to call you Super Stink," said Sophie of the Elves.

"Then I'll have to call you Sophie of the Smells!"

"Hey, no fair," said Webster. "You're Super Stink, and she's Sophie of the Smells. I want a smelly name, too."

"Hmm. Webster. How about . . . The Smellster?" said Stink.

"Perfect!" said The Smellster.

"Now all your friends are smelly, Stink," said Judy.

"How'd you get the name Stink, anyway?" asked Sophie of the Smells.

"HER," said Stink, pointing to Judy.

"I'll tell it! I'll tell it!" Judy said. "See, when Stink was a baby, Dad started calling him Peanut. I was jealous, because Dad had always called *me* Peanut. So I tried to think up a new name. Then one day, Dad was changing Stink's dirty diaper . . ."

"Eee-yew!" said Webster, pinching his nose.

"If you want to be a Master Sniffer, you have to be able to smell dirty diapers," said Stink. "Professor Steve said so."

"Okay, Professor Smells-Himself-a-Lot," said Judy. "Anyway, it was really stinky. So I started singing this song I learned in preschool."

"Don't sing it!" said Stink, covering his ears.

"Sing it!" said Webster and Sophie.

"It sounds like 'Old McDonald Had a Farm.'

My little brother smells so bad,
Stinky, stinky poo!

With a stink, stink here
And a stink, stink there.
Here a stink,
There a stink,
Everywhere a stink, stink!

My little brother smells so bad,
Stinky, stinky poo!

POP

Sophie of the Smells and The Smellster joined in on the last verse. Sophie sprayed soda on Stink from laughing. Webster was clutching his stomach and rolling on the floor.

"Ever since then, we called him Stinky Poo," said Judy.

"Then one day, it got shortened to just plain Stink," said Stink.

"And now, Super Stink," said Sophie and Webster.

Super Stink couldn't help smiling. Today had given him a brand-new smellosophy of life.

* * *

That night, as Stink drifted off to sleep, visions of corpse flowers danced in his head. Rumpel-STINK-skin, Stink "The Nose" Moody, Way-Official Junior Sniffer, was on his way!

Megan McDonald

is the author of the popular series starring Judy Moody. She says, "Once, while I was visiting a class, the kids chanted, 'Stink! Stink! Stink!' as I entered the room. In that moment, I knew that Stink had to have a book all his own." Megan McDonald lives in California.

Peter H. Reynolds

is the illustrator of all the Judy Moody books. He says, "Stink reminds me of myself growing up: dealing with a sister prone to teasing and bossing around—and having to get creative in order to stand tall beside her." Peter H. Reynolds lives in Massachusetts.

Be sure to check out

Stink's adventures!

Don't miss Stink's next out-of-this-world adventure!

When Stink learns that Pluto has flunked out of the Milky Way for being too shrimpy, he has no choice but to take a stand for the sake of little planets (and little people) everywhere.

Think you know Stink?

Stink-o-pedia

Super Stink-y Stuff from A to Zzzzz